Black Beauty

Beauty

黑駿馬

商務印書館

Name of Book: Black Beauty
Author: Anna Sewell
Editor: Michela Bruzzo
Design and art direction: Nadia Maestri
Computer graphics: Simona Corniola
Picture research: Laura Lagomarsino
Edition: ©2007 Black Cat Publishing,
　　　　　an imprint of Cideb Editrice, Genoa, Canterbury

系 列 名：Black Cat 優質英語階梯閱讀 · Level 1
書　　名：黑駿馬
責任編輯：畢　琦
封面設計：張　毅
出　　版：商務印書館（香港）有限公司
　　　　　香港筲箕灣耀興道 3 號東滙廣場 8 樓
　　　　　http://www.commercialpress.com.hk
發　　行：香港聯合書刊物流有限公司
　　　　　香港新界大埔汀麗路 36 號中華商務印刷大廈 3 字樓
印　　刷：中華商務彩色印刷有限公司
　　　　　香港新界大埔汀麗路 36 號中華商務印刷大廈
版　　次：2008 年 6 月第 1 版第 1 次印刷
　　　　　© 2008 商務印書館（香港）有限公司
　　　　　ISBN 978 962 07 1843 4
　　　　　Printed in Hong Kong

版權所有　不得翻印

出版說明

　　本館一向倡導優質閱讀，近年來連續推出了以"Q"為標識的"Quality English Learning 優質英語學習"系列，其中《讀名著學英語》叢書，更是香港書展入選好書，讀者反響令人鼓舞。推動社會閱讀風氣，推動英語經典閱讀，藉閱讀拓廣世界視野，提高英語水平，已經成為一種潮流。

　　然良好閱讀習慣的養成非一日之功，大多數初中級程度的讀者，常視直接閱讀厚重的原著為畏途。如何給年輕的讀者提供切實的指引和幫助，如何既提供優質的學習素材，又提供名師的教學方法，是當下社會關注的重要問題。針對這種情況，本館特別延請香港名校名師，根據多年豐富的教學經驗，精選海外適合初中級英語程度讀者的優質經典讀物，有系統地出版了這套叢書，名為《Black Cat 優質英語階梯閱讀》。

　　《Black Cat 優質英語階梯閱讀》體現了香港名校名師堅持經典學習的教學理念，以及多年行之有效的學習方法。既有經過改寫和縮寫的經典名著，又有富創意的現代作品；既有精心設計的聽、說、讀、寫綜合練習，又有豐富的歷史文化知識；既有彩色插圖、繪圖和照片，又有英美專業演員朗讀作品的 CD。適合口味不同的讀者享受閱讀之樂，欣賞經典之美。

　　《Black Cat 優質英語階梯閱讀》由淺入深，逐階提升，好像參與一個尋寶遊戲，入門並不難，但要真正尋得寶藏，需要投入，更需要堅持。只有置身其中的人，才能體味純正英語的魅力，領略得到真寶的快樂。當英語閱讀成為自己生活的一部分，英語水平的提高自然水到渠成。

商務印書館（香港）有限公司
編輯部

使用說明

❶ 應該怎樣選書？

按閱讀興趣選書

《Black Cat 優質英語階梯閱讀》精選世界經典作品，也包括富於創意的現代作品；既有膾炙人口的小說、戲劇，又有非小說類的文化知識讀物，品種豐富，內容多樣，適合口味不同的讀者挑選自己感興趣的書，享受閱讀的樂趣。

按英語程度選書

《Black Cat 優質英語階梯閱讀》現設 Level 1 至 Level 6，由淺入深，涵蓋初、中級英語程度。讀物分級採用了國際上通用的劃分標準，主要以詞彙（vocabulary）和結構（structures）劃分。

Level 1 至 Level 3 出現的詞彙較淺顯，相對深的核心詞彙均配上中文解釋，節省讀者查找詞典的時間，以專心理解正文內容。在註釋的幫助下，讀者若能流暢地閱讀正文內容，就不用擔心這本書程度過深。

Level 1 至 Level 3 出現的動詞時態形式和句子結構比較簡單。動詞時態形式以簡單現在式（present simple）、現在進行式（present continuous）、簡單過去式（past simple）為主，句子結構大部分是簡單句（simple sentences）。此外，還包括比較級和最高級（comparative and superlative forms）、可數和不可數名詞（countable and uncountable nouns）以及冠詞（articles）等語法知識點。

Level 4 至 Level 6 出現的動詞時態形式，以現在完成式（present perfect）、現在完成進行式（present perfect continuous）、過去完成進行式（past perfect continuous）為主，句子結構大部分是複合句（compound sentences）、條件從句（1st and 2nd conditional sentences）等。此外，還包括情態動詞（modal verbs）、被動式（passive forms）、動名詞（gerunds）、短

語動詞（phrasal verbs）等語法知識點。

　　根據上述的語法範圍，讀者可按自己實際的英語水平，如詞彙量、語法知識、理解能力、閱讀能力等自主選擇，不再受制於學校年級劃分或學歷高低的約束，完全根據個人需要選擇合適的讀物。

② 怎樣提高閱讀效果？

　　閱讀的方法主要有兩種：一是泛讀，二是精讀。兩者各有功能，適當地結合使用，相輔相成，有事半功倍之效。

　　泛讀，指閱讀大量適合自己程度（可稍淺，但不能過深）、不同內容、風格、體裁的讀物，但求明白內容大意，不用花費太多時間鑽研細節，主要作用是多接觸英語，減輕對它的生疏感，鞏固以前所學過的英語，讓腦子在潛意識中吸收詞彙用法、語法結構等。

　　精讀，指小心認真地閱讀內容精彩、組織有條理、遣詞造句又正確的作品，着重點在於理解“準確”及“深入”，欣賞其精彩獨到之處。精讀時，可充分利用書中精心設計的練習，學習掌握有用的英語詞彙和語法知識。精讀後，可再花十分鐘朗讀其中一小段有趣的文字，邊唸邊細心領會文字的結構和意思。

　　《Black Cat 優質英語階梯閱讀》中的作品均值得精讀，如時間有限，不妨嘗試每兩個星期泛讀一本，輔以每星期挑選書中一章精彩的文字精讀。要學好英語，持之以恆地泛讀和精讀英文是最有效的方法。

③ 本系列的練習與測試有何功能？

　　《Black Cat 優質英語階梯閱讀》特別注重練習的設計，為讀者考慮周到，切合實用需求，學習功能強。每章後均配有訓練聽、說、讀、寫四項技能的練習，分量、難度恰到好處。

聽力練習分兩類，一是重聽故事回答問題，二是聆聽主角對話、書信朗讀、或模擬記者訪問後寫出答案，旨在以生活化的練習形式逐步提高聽力。每本書均配有CD提供作品朗讀，朗讀者都是專業演員，英國作品由英國演員錄音，美國作品由美國演員錄音，務求增加聆聽的真實感和感染力。多聆聽英式和美式英語兩種發音，可讓讀者熟悉二者的差異，逐漸培養分辨英美發音的能力，提高聆聽理解的準確度。此外，模仿錄音朗讀故事或模仿主人翁在戲劇中的對白，都是訓練口語能力的好方法。

閱讀理解練習形式多樣化，有縱橫字謎、配對、填空、字句重組等等，注重訓練讀者的理解、推敲和聯想等多種閱讀技能。

寫作練習尤具新意，教讀者使用網式圖示（spidergrams）記錄重點，採用問答、書信、電報、記者採訪等多樣化形式，鼓勵讀者動手寫作。

書後更設有升級測試（Exit Test）及答案，供讀者檢查學習效果。充分利用書中的練習和測試，可全面提升聽、說、讀、寫四項技能。

◆4 本系列還能提供甚麼幫助？

《Black Cat 優質英語階梯閱讀》提倡豐富多元的現代閱讀，巧用書中提供的資訊，有助於提升英語理解力，擴闊視野。

每本書都設有專章介紹相關的歷史文化知識，經典名著更附有作者生平、社會背景等資訊。書內富有表現力的彩色插圖、繪圖和照片，使閱讀充滿趣味，部分加上如何解讀古典名畫的指導，增長見識。有的書還提供一些與主題相關的網址，比如關於不同國家的節慶源流的網址，讓讀者多利用網上資源增進知識。

Contents

The text is recorded in full.   全文錄音

 END   These symbols indicate the beginning and end of the extracts linked to the listening activities.   聽力練習開始和結束的標記

Anna Sewell, from the frontispiece of *Black Beauty*, published by Harrap.

Let's meet Anna Sewell

Name: Anna Sewell

Born: Norfolk, England

When: 20 March 1820

Important event in her life: at the age of 14 she falls, hurts her legs and cannot walk well. She always rides a horse to get around. She loves horses.

Her only book: *Black Beauty* (1877)

Died: 1878

The Characters

Captain

Lizzie

Max

Ginger

Duchess

Marrylegs

Black Beauty

BEFORE YOU READ

SETTING

Match these words to the things and the animals in the picture. Use a dictionary.

1 meadow   2 colt   3 oats   4 carriage   5 hare   6 hunting dogs
7 gun   8 black coat   9 cow   10 sheep   11 saddle   12 bridle
13 bit   14 horseshoes   15 stall   16 stable   17 pond

2 CROSSWORD

Across

3

8

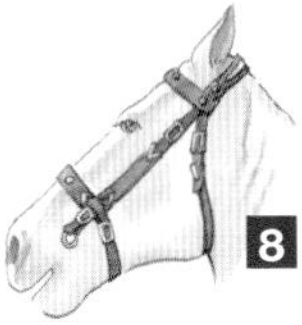

9

11

14

15

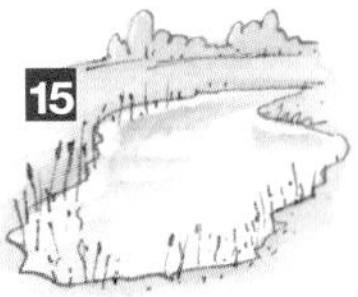

16

Down

1

2

4

5

7

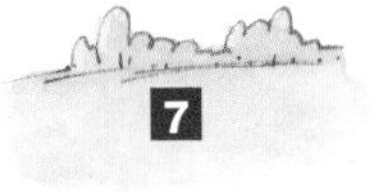

10

12

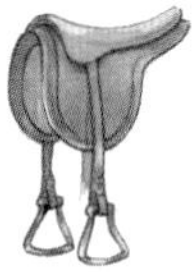

13

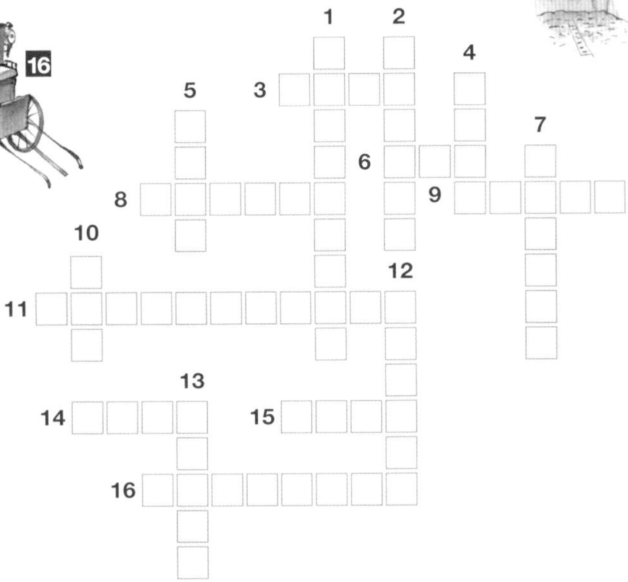

CHAPTER ONE

My First Home

I live in a big meadow with a pond and trees around it. During the day I run in the meadow with my mother and at night I sleep next to her.

There are six other colts in the meadow. I run with them too and have great fun. But sometimes they kick and bite me [1].

My mother always says, 'These colts are good but they're not polite. You come from a family of famous horses. You must always be good and gentle [2], and never bite or kick.'

My mother's name is Duchess and she is old and wise [3]. She is our master's favourite horse and she always takes him to town in a small carriage. Our master is a kind man. He gives us a lot of oats, a big carrot and a warm place to live. He always says nice things to us. Sometimes he gives us some sugar. We all love him.

1. **kick and bite me**：踢我和咬我。
2. **be good and gentle**：和藹可親的。
3. **wise**：有智慧的。

One day I see a lot of dogs running in another green meadow and they are barking [1] loudly.

'What's happening, mother?' I ask.

'The dogs are running after a hare,' she says. 'There is a hunt.'

The dogs run fast and the hare does, too. There is a lot of noise. Finally the dogs catch the poor hare and kill it. Then another sad thing happens. Two horses and two men fall to the ground. One man gets up but the other does not. The dogs are silent now, and everyone is looking at the man and the two horses.

'It's young George Gordon, the landowner's [2] son,' says mother sadly. 'The poor young man is dead.'

1. **barking**：犬吠。
2. **landowner**：地主。

Only one horse gets up but the other cannot because his leg is broken. Someone runs to the master's house and gets a gun. There is a loud shot [1] and the horse is dead.

I am four years old now and I am a handsome [2] colt. I have a nice black coat and a white star on my forehead [3]. One day the landowner, Mr Gordon, comes to look at me. He looks at my eyes, my teeth and my legs.

'When you break him in [4], I want to see him,' says Mr Gordon.

1. **shot** : 槍聲。
2. **handsome** : 英俊的。
3. **forehead** : 前額。
4. **break him in** : 第一次試騎。

15

'Very well, Mr Gordon,' says my master. He smiles at me and says, 'Tomorrow I must break you in. I must teach you to wear a saddle and bridle and carry a person on your back. Then I must teach you to pull a carriage.'

'Tomorrow is an important day,' says mother quietly. 'Remember, you must always listen to your master, and never bite or kick. And you must never jump when you're happy or stop when you're tired. Always be a good horse.'

The next day my master comes and talks to me quietly. Then he gently [1] puts the bit into my mouth and the bridle on my face. The bit hurts my mouth and feels terrible, but my mother and other adult [2] horses wear it too.

Then my master puts a saddle on my back and says kind words to me. He slowly gets on the saddle and rides me around the meadow. I am happy when I carry him.

After some time he takes me

1. **gently**：輕柔地。
2. **adult**：成年的。

to the blacksmith [1]. The blacksmith puts on horseshoes. They are very heavy metal shoes and I do not like them.

'Today we're going to visit my friend Simon,' my master says. At Simon's house I stay in a meadow with cows and sheep. Suddenly a big train goes by and it makes a lot of noise and smoke. I run to the other side of the meadow because I am afraid, but the cows and sheep do

1. **blacksmith** : 鐵匠。

not move. A lot of trains go by, but they do not hurt me so I am not afraid of them.

Sometimes I pull the carriage with my mother and she teaches me a lot of things. 'There are many kinds of masters,' she says. Some are good, but others are bad and cruel [1]. You must always listen to them, and remember the good name of your family.'

In May, one of Mr Gordon's men comes and takes me away. My master says, 'Goodbye, my friend. Be a good horse and always do your best.' I cannot say goodbye, so I put my nose in his hand.

My new home at Mr Gordon's is lovely. There is a big stable and I have a comfortable stall.

There is another horse in the next stall. 'Hello, what's your name?' I ask.

'My name is Merrylegs,' says the horse. 'I carry the young ladies on my back. Are you my new neighbour [2]?'

'Yes, I am.'

'Do you bite?' asks Merrylegs.

'No, I don't,' I answer. 'I only bite grass.'

'Oh, good, because the horse in the other stall sometimes bites,' says Merrylegs. 'She's a brown horse and her name is Ginger.'

1. **cruel** : 殘忍。
2. **neighbour** : 鄰居。

UNDERSTANDING THE TEXT

 COMPREHENSION CHECK

Are these sentences 'Right' (A) or 'Wrong'(B)? If there is not enough information to answer 'Right' (A) or 'Wrong' (B), choose 'Doesn't say' (C). There is an example at the beginning (0).

0 Black Beauty lives in the woods near a river.
   A Right   Ⓑ Wrong   C Doesn't say

1 His mother is a big black horse.
   A Right   B Wrong   C Doesn't say

2 A horse breaks his leg during a hunt.
   A Right   B Wrong   C Doesn't say

3 George Gordon is twenty-one years old.
   A Right   B Wrong   C Doesn't say

4 Black Beauty has a black coat and a brown star on his forehead.
   A Right   B Wrong   C Doesn't say

5 Mr Gordon teaches the colt to wear a saddle and bridle.
   A Right   B Wrong   C Doesn't say

6 Black Beauty doesn't like the bit because it hurts his mouth.
   A Right   B Wrong   C Doesn't say

7 He doesn't like carrying the master.
   A Right   B Wrong   C Doesn't say

8 The blacksmith's name is Simon Brown.
   A Right   B Wrong   C Doesn't say

9 Black Beauty is afraid of the train and runs to the other side of the meadow.
   A Right   B Wrong   C Doesn't say

10 Merrylegs and Ginger are Mr Gordon's horses.
   A Right   B Wrong   C Doesn't say

11 Black Beauty is Merrylegs's new neighbour.
   A Right   B Wrong   C Doesn't say

12 Ginger never bites.
   A Right   B Wrong   C Doesn't say

2 ▶ VOCABULARY
Can you remember these words from the setting on pages 10 and 11? Complete the sentences.

1 Duchess takes the master to town in a small ....
2 There is another .... in the meadow.
3 Black Beauty wears a .... on his back.
4 Black Beauty wears a .... on his head and a .... in his mouth.
5 The .... puts .... on his feet.
6 The horses live inside a big ....
7 Black Beauty has a comfortable .... next to Merrylegs.

3 ▶ Now find the words in the word square and circle them in red.

```
M B A P V O F S R N C M H Z
O B L S B R I D L E D L O B
P Y L A G S E V M W L P R S
C S F A C B L A Z A J R S A
F O B V L K O S T A B L E D
W M L R M Y S O N U R C S D
Z P U T X C T M Y T V R H L
C A R R I A G E I B P M O E
U O I F Z P R B S T R D E O
I Y A S T A L L C B H J S X
```

T: GRADE 2
4 ▶ SPEAKING: ANIMALS AND PETS
Black Beauty **is a story about horses. Bring in a picture of your favourite animal or pet and talk about it. Use these questions to help you.**

1 What's its name?
2 How old is it?
3 Describe it (colour, size).
4 Does it live outside or in a house?
5 What does it eat?

'HE GIVES US …A BIG CARROT. SOMETIMES HE GIVES US SOME SUGAR.'

Some nouns（名詞）have got singular and plural forms（單數和複數形式）. You can count them. These are **countable nouns**（可數名詞）.

Examples: *a carrot, three carrots*

　　　　　a horse, two horses

Some nouns have got only one form. These are **uncountable nouns**（不可數名詞）. We can say 'a glass of water' but we cannot say 'a water'.

Examples: *some sugar, some water*

 5 COUNTABLE AND UNCOUNTABLE NOUNS
Look at the words below. Which have got plural forms（複數形式）and which haven't? Write the words in the correct column.

milk　　carrot　　rain　　money　　apple　　butter　　egg .
cake　　meat　　orange　　bread　　music　　banana
cow　　horseshoe　　grass

COUNTABLE	UNCOUNTABLE
....	....
....	....
....	....
....	....
....	....
....	....
....	....

BEFORE YOU READ

1 READING PICTURES
Look at the picture on pages 24 and 25. Then answer these questions.

1　What time of day is it?
2　What's the weather like?
3　Who is on the bridge?
4　What is he doing and why?
5　Who is in the carriage?
6　Why is Black Beauty stopping?

◆ VOCABULARY

Match each word with a picture.

coachman   whip   blanket   gallop   bridge   bell

1

2

3

4

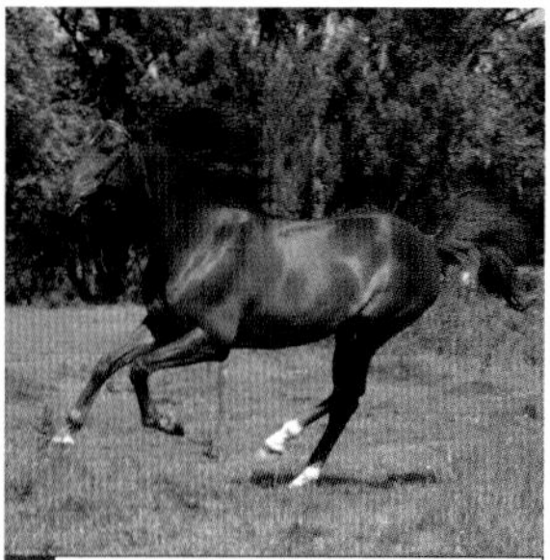

5

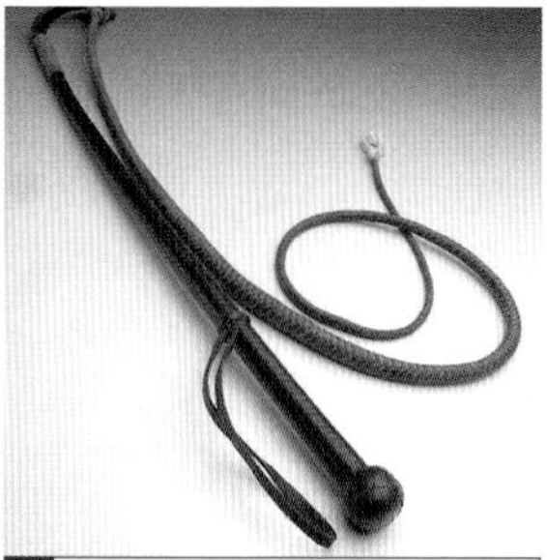

6

◆ LISTENING

Listen to the first part of Chapter Two. Are these sentences true (T) or false (F)?

		T	F
1	John Manly is a good rider.	☐	☐
2	He lives in the stable with the horses.	☐	☐
3	The colt's new name is Black Beauty.	☐	☐
4	Sometimes Ginger bites and kicks.	☐	☐
5	Ginger is not happy with John and Mr Gordon.	☐	☐
6	Ginger and Black Beauty become good friends.	☐	☐
7	Merrylegs is Mr Gordon's favourite horse.	☐	☐
8	Flora and Jessie are Mr Gordon's daughters.	☐	☐

CHAPTER TWO

The Bridge

y coachman [1]'s name is John Manly and he lives near the stables. John is a friendly man and he always gives me a good grooming [2]. He is a good rider too.

'Good morning, John,' says Mr Gordon. 'How's the new horse?'

'He's fast and easy to ride, sir,' says John. 'He comes from a good family.'

'What's his name?' asks Mr Gordon.

'I don't know, sir,' says John.

'Well, he's a beauty [3],' says Mr Gordon, 'Let's call him Black Beauty.'

I like my new name and my new master.

After a few days John says to me, 'Today you're going out in a carriage with Ginger.'

I am not happy about this because Ginger is not friendly [4]. But after a few rides in the carriage we start talking.

---

1. **coachman**：馬夫。
2. **he always gives me a good grooming**：他總是讓我梳洗一新。
3. **beauty**：美人。
4. **friendly**：友好的。

'Sometimes I bite and kick, but I'm not a bad horse,' says Ginger sadly. 'In my life I can only remember cruel masters, bad coachmen and the whip [1].'

'Oh, I'm sorry, Ginger,' I say. 'Are you happy here?'

'Yes, I am,' says Ginger, 'because the master and the coachman are both kind. They understand horses.'

Now we are good friends and I like her a lot. I also like Merrylegs because he is always happy and friendly. He is the favourite [2] horse of Miss Jessie and Flora. They are Mr Gordon's daughters.

END

One cloudy autumn day the master says, 'John, get the carriage ready with Black Beauty. We must go to town on business [3].' This is the first time for me to go to town with the master and John. I am excited [4]. I want to do my best and please the master.

1. **whip**：鞭子。
2. **favourite**：最喜愛的。
3. **business**：公務。
4. **excited**：興奮的。

The master and John are in the carriage, and it starts raining and it is very windy. We get to town and the master goes to see some people. John and I wait for him in the rain.

When he finishes his business he says, 'Let's go home, John. Perhaps we can cross the bridge before it is dark.'

'It's a dangerous [1] bridge when it rains,' says John.

We take the country road to the bridge and it is raining hard. I am very careful because the road is bad. When my feet touch [2] the bridge I know something is wrong. I cannot move and I stop.

1. **dangerous** : 危險的。
2. **touch** : 接觸。

'Go on, Black Beauty,' says my master.

I cannot move because I feel there is danger on the bridge.

'There's something wrong, sir,' says John. 'Beauty doesn't want to cross the bridge.'

'But we must cross the bridge. It's late,' says the master.

At that moment a man runs out of his house and cries, 'Stop! Stop! Go back! Don't cross the bridge. It's broken in the middle.'

'Broken in the middle?' says the master. 'Oh, thank you, Black Beauty.'

'Yes, thank you, Beauty,' says John.

We take another country road and get home late.

'What a rainy night!' says the mistress [1] when she sees us. 'I'm happy you're home.'

'You can thank Black Beauty. He's a very wise horse,' says the master.

That night John dries my wet coat and puts on my warm blue blanket [2]. Then he gives me a good dinner and I can finally sleep.

The next day a new stable boy comes to work. His name is Joe Green and he is fourteen years old. I like him because he has a gentle hand and he talks to me.

One night the stable bell rings loudly and all the horses wake up. I hear John's voice. 'Beauty, wake up. The mistress is very ill and we must go and find Doctor White.'

He puts a saddle on my back and gets on. I gallop [3] fast because I want to help the mistress. It is a dark, cold night.

When we get to Doctor White's house, John calls him. A

---

1. **mistress**：女主人。
2. **blanket**：毛毯。
3. **gallop**：飛跑。

window opens and the doctor puts his head out and says, 'What's the matter at three o'clock in the morning?'

'Mrs Gordon is very ill,' says John. 'Please come at once.'

'Can I use your horse?' asks the doctor. 'My horse has a bad leg.'

'Yes, of course,' says John.

The doctor is a heavy man and not a good rider. But I do my best and gallop home. He runs to see the mistress and Joe takes me to the stable. I am very wet and cold. Joe dries me and gives me some water and oats [1]. But he forgets to put my warm blue blanket on. Soon I start shaking [2] and I am very cold. I feel terrible.

The next day the master comes to see me.

'Thanks to you, Black Beauty, the mistress is feeling better,' he says. 'But now you are ill, my poor Beauty. We must call the vet [3] at once.'

I am very ill now, but the master's kind words make me feel better.

---

1. **oats**：燕麥。
2. **shaking**：冷得發抖。
3. **vet**：獸醫（veterinarian 的縮寫）。

UNDERSTANDING THE TEXT

KET

1 COMPREHENSION CHECK

Choose the correct answer (A, B or C). There is an example at the beginning (0).

0 John Manly is

   A ☐ Mr Gordon's best friend.

   B ☑ Black Beauty's coachman.

   C ☐ the blacksmith.

1 Ginger can only remember

   A ☐ kind masters and warm stables.

   B ☐ good riders and friendly children.

   C ☐ cruel masters and their whips.

2 One day the master wants to go

   A ☐ to London with his wife.

   B ☐ to town on business.

   C ☐ to church with his family.

3 Black Beauty does not want to cross the bridge

   A ☐ and runs away into the forest.

   B ☐ because he is afraid.

   C ☐ because he knows something is wrong.

4 The new stable boy is

   A ☐ Joe Green: he is fourteen years old.

   B ☐ Joe White: he is cruel.

   C ☐ Joe: he is Mr Manly's son.

5 One cold night Black Beauty takes John

   A ☐ to Doctor Gordon's house.

   B ☐ to the village.

   C ☐ to Doctor White's house.

6 The master calls the vet

   A ☐ and they have dinner together.

   B ☐ because Black Beauty is ill.

   C ☐ because the mistress is ill.

② FILL IN THE GAPS

Complete this postcard Mr Gordon writes to his brother. Write one word in each space (1-9). There is an example at the beginning (0).

Dear Thomas,

I have (0) .....a............... new horse. (1) .... name is Black Beauty and he (2) .... handsome. He (3) .... a black coat and a white star (4) .... his forehead. He comes (5) .... a good family (6) .... he is gentle.

Now I have ten horses (7) .... my stable. Tomorrow I (8) .... going to town (9) .... Black Beauty for the first time. I (10) .... you can come and see my new horse and me soon.

Your brother,

Richard

③ VOCABULARY

Circle the word that does not belong.

1 train   carriage   boat   bus
2 gallop   run   walk   sleep
3 autumn   month   spring   summer
4 neighbour   doctor   blacksmith   coachman
5 road   street   path   bridge

Now complete each sentence with the word that does not belong.

1 January is the first .... of the year.
2 The horses .... in the stable at night.
3 Black Beauty doesn't want to cross the ....
4 Flora is playing with a toy .... by the river.
5 Merrylegs is Black Beauty's ....

④ CHARACTERS

Circle the words that describe John Manly.

old	friendly	kind	cruel	fat	good
understanding	tall	good rider	coachman		

Now write a sentence about John Manly using some of the words above.

....

5 ► IDENTITY CARD
Fill in Black Beauty's ID card.

My name is (1)............................. .
My coat is (2).............. and I have a
(3)......................... on my forehead.
I live in a (4)................................ .
My master is (5)............................ .
My coachman is (6) ....
I like eating (7).............................. .
My friends are (8) ....
and (9)... .

KET

6 ► CONVERSATION
Complete the conversation. What does the master say to John? For questions (1-5), write the correct letter (A-H). There is an example at the beginning (0).

Master: John, get the carriage ready!
John: 0 ....E.....
Master: I want to go to town. What time is it now?
John: 1 ....
Master: It's very late. The shops close at five. Let's take the road near the old bridge.
John: 2 ....
Master: I know, but it's a fast road. Is the carriage ready now?
John: 3 ....
Master: Oh, I forgot my coat. Please go and get it.
John: 4 ....
Master: It's on the big chair in the kitchen.
John: 5 ....

A Who is it?
B I can't find it.
C Where do you go?
D It's half past three.

E Where are we going?
F But it's dangerous.
G Where is it?
H Yes, it is.

31

BEFORE YOU READ

READING PICTURES

Look at the picture on pages 34 and 35 and answer the following questions.

1 What is the man doing?
2 Where is Black Beauty?

Now look at the picture on pages 36 and 37 and answer the following questions.

1 What are the horses doing?
2 What is one man trying to do to Ginger?
3 How does the lady in the carriage feel, and why?
4 What is the house like?

LISTENING

Listen to the first part of Chapter Three and choose the correct answer (A, B or C).

1 Who is ill?
    A ☐ the master
    B ☐ the mistress
    C ☐ Black Beauty

2 Where must the mistress go?
    A ☐ to a warm country
    B ☐ to a cold country
    C ☐ to London

3 Who hugs Merrylegs?
    A ☐ the old Vicar
    B ☐ the master
    C ☐ Jessie and Flora

4 Where does Lord Wadsworth live?
    A ☐ near the river
    B ☐ in the country
    C ☐ in the city

5 Who is the new coachman?
    A ☐ Mr York
    B ☐ John Manly
    C ☐ Lord Wadsworth

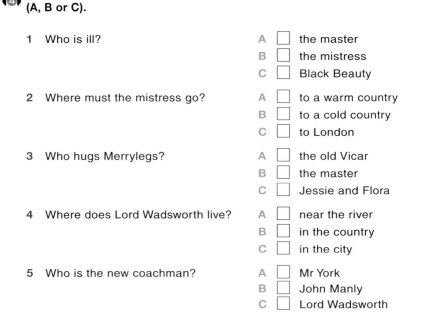

Lord and Lady Wadsworth

My life at Mr Gordon's is happy but things are changing. The mistress is ill and the master is sad and worried.

Doctor White comes here often and says, 'Mrs Gordon must go to a warm country for two or three years. Then perhaps she can get better.'

Everyone is sad because we must soon say goodbye.

One day Jessie and Flora come to the stable.

'Goodbye, dear Merrylegs,' they say. 'Thank you for all the wonderful rides.' They hug him like an old friend.

'Don't be sad, Merrylegs,' says Jessie, 'father is selling you to the old Vicar [1]. He is a kind man and loves horses.'

Then the master comes to the stable and talks to Ginger and me.

---

1. **Vicar**：教區牧師。

'I'm selling you to Lord Wadsworth. He's a good man and lives in the country. Goodbye, Black Beauty and Ginger.' He pats [1] us on the neck for a long time. I cannot say goodbye so I put my nose in his hand. Ginger and I are very sad to leave our master and our stable. But this is the life of a horse.

Lord Wadsworth has a beautiful house with a green meadow and big stables. John and our new coachman, Mr York, take us to our stalls.

He looks at us carefully [2] and says, 'They look like very good horses, Mr Manly. What can you tell me about them?'

'Black Beauty is gentle and wise, and always does his best,' says John. 'He is also very fast.

END

1. **pats** : 輕拍。
2. **carefully** : 仔細地。

Ginger's a good horse too, but sometimes she's nervous [1].'

'Do they wear the bearing rein [2]?' asks Mr York.

'No, they don't,' says John.

'Well,' says Mr York, 'here they must wear it. The lord and I like a soft rein, but Lady Wadsworth wants the bearing rein. The horses must keep their heads high.'

'Horses don't like it,' says John. 'It's very uncomfortable [3] and it hurts their head and neck.'

'You're right,' says Mr York, 'but the lady isn't kind.'

I do not know what a bearing rein is, but it sounds terrible.

The next day Ginger and I pull the lady's carriage and we must wear it. It is very uncomfortable because we cannot put our heads down. It is a cruel thing for a horse.

'I hate the bearing rein,' says Ginger one evening. 'My head, neck and mouth hurt terribly. People don't wear it so they can't understand [4].'

'I hate it too,' I say, 'but what can a poor horse do?'

'We can do nothing, Beauty,' says Ginger sadly.

1. **nervous** : 緊張的。
2. **bearing rein** : 頸韁，揹壓韁。
3. **uncomfortable** : 難受的。
4. **understand** : 理解。

We wear the bearing rein every day.

The lady comes down the stairs in a beautiful dress and says, 'York, take me to the Duchess of Barstow. And I want the horses' heads high – very high.' She gets into the carriage and sits down. York prepares Ginger and me. He comes to me first and pulls the bearing rein – it feels terrible. Then he goes to Ginger and does the same. Ginger gets angry and starts kicking wildly [1]. York falls to the ground and the lady in the carriage screams [2].

1. **wildly** : 狂野地。
2. **screams** : 尖叫。

Two grooms [1] come from the stable and take poor Ginger away. She does not ride with me anymore. The master uses her for the hunts because she is fast. My new carriage partner is Max, a quiet, grey horse.

I think about my old home a lot. Here I have food and a clean stall, but I don't have a lot of friends. York is a good man but he is not my friend.

1. **grooms** : 馬夫。

UNDERSTANDING THE TEXT

 SUMMARY

Read the summary of Chapter Three. Choose the best word (A, B or C) for each space (1-12). There is an example at the beginning (0).

Mrs Gordon is ill and she must go to a warm country. Squire Gordon (0) ..A... Black Beauty and Ginger (1) ...... Lord Wadsworth. He is a good man.

Flora and Jessie go to the stable and say goodbye to Merrylegs.

The horses are sad when they leave (2) ...... master.

Lord Wadsworth has a lovely house in the country. There is a big green meadow. Lady Wadsworth wants the horses to (3) ...... the bearing rein, because their heads must be (4) ....

Black Beauty and Ginger do not like the bearing rein (5) ...... it hurts their head and neck. They are unhappy.

One day Lady Wadsworth goes to visit the Duchess of Barstow. The horses must wear the bearing rein. York puts the bearing rein on Black Beauty first. Then he puts it on Ginger. She (6) ...... kicking and York falls (7) ...... the ground. The lady in (8) ...... carriage screams. Two grooms take Ginger away. She does not pull the carriage (9) ...... Black Beauty anymore. Max is Black Beauty's new carriage partner. (10) ...... is a quiet horse.

Black Beauty thinks (11) ...... his old home and his old friends. York is a good man but he is not (12) ...... friend.

0	Ⓐ sells	B buys	C gives
1	A for	B at	C to
2	A their	B there	C they're
3	A wear	B were	C where
4	A tall	B high	C top
5	A so	B why	C because
6	A start	B starts	C starting
7	A to	B at	C in
8	A a	B one	C the
9	A with	B together	C along
10	A Him	B His	C He
11	A on	B about	C at
12	A his	B he	C its

2 VOCABULARY

Match the opposites（反義詞）.

1	☐	sad	A	uncomfortable
2	☐	fast	B	push
3	☐	comfortable	C	dirty
4	☐	cruel	D	slow
5	☐	pull	E	loud
6	☐	high	F	happy
7	☐	quiet	G	kind
8	☐	clean	H	low

Now write four sentences using some of the adjectives（形容詞）above.

1 ....

2 ....

3 ....

4 ....

KET

3 VOCABULARY

Read the definitions (1-9) of some words. What is the word for each one? The first letter is already there. There is one space for each letter in the word. There is an example at the beginning (0).

0	heavy metal shoes	h _o_ _r_ _s_ _e_ _s_ _h_ _o_ _e_ _s_
1	a big house for horses	s _ _ _ _ _
2	a young horse	c _ _ _
3	horses eat these	o _ _ _
4	you use it to sit on a horse	s _ _ _ _ _
5	you use it to shoot	g _ _
6	it keeps you warm	b _ _ _ _ _
7	to touch gently	p _ _
8	this doctor looks after animals	v _ _
9	very unkind	c _ _ _ _

4 NOTICES

Which notice (A-H) says this (1-5)? There is an example at the beginning (0).

A

Do not take horses off the footpath

B

Train for London on platform 3

C

Hire a carriage every day from 8 am to 7 pm except Sundays

D

Horses not allowed in St James's Park on Sundays

E

Private property No trespassing!

F

St James's Art Museum Closed 24 - 26 December

G

Restaurant and gift shop at the zoo entrance

H

SALLY'S SPORTS SHOP
50% OFF ON ALL
RIDING EQUIPMENT

0 ...B... Catch the train for London on platform 3

1 ...... You can ride your horse in St James's Park on Tuesday.

2 ...... You can't hire a carriage here at 9 pm.

3 ...... You can eat lunch at the zoo.

4 ...... You can't visit the museum at Christmas.

5 ...... You can't enter here.

The Royal Society¹ for the Prevention² of Cruelty to Animals

In the 1800s animals are often  mistreated ³ by cruel owners, and no one protects ⁴ them. In 1824 Richard Martin opens the Society for the Prevention of Cruelty to Animals in London. It is the first national animal protection society in the world. In 1840 Queen Victoria gives her permission ⁵ to call it the Royal Society for the Prevention of Cruelty to Animals (the RSPCA ⁶). People begin to understand that animals are living creatures and it is wrong to mistreat them.

Today the RSPCA is an important organisation with more than 400 inspectors. They visit homes, pet shops, farms and laboratories. They work with schools to teach kindness towards animals. They also work with the government to pass laws

The RSPCA also inspects animals in circuses.

1. **Society** : 協會。
2. **Prevention** : 防止。
3. **mistreated** : 虐待。
4. **protects** : 保護。
5. **permission** : 允許。
6. **RSPCA** : 皇家防止虐待動物協會。

that protect animals. The RSPCA has animal hospitals and centres for abandoned [1] animals all over England and Wales.

1. **abandoned** : 遭到遺棄的。

Orphan kitten drinking milk from a bottle.

1 **COMPREHENSION CHECK**
Are these sentences true (T) or false (F)? Correct the false ones.

		T	F
1	Queen Victoria opens the Society for the Prevention of Cruelty to Animals in 1824.	☐	☐
2	In 1840 Queen Victoria gives her permission to call it the Royal Society for the Prevention of Cruelty to Animals.	☐	☐
3	Today there are more than one hundred inspectors in the RSPCA.	☐	☐
4	They help and protect animals in zoos.	☐	☐
5	The RSPCA has animal hospitals and centres for abandoned animals in England and Wales.	☐	☐

PROJECT ON THE WEB

Connect to the Internet and go to www.blackcat-cideb.com or www.cideb.it. Insert the title or part of the title of the book into our search engine. Open the page for *Black Beauty*. Click on the Internet project link. Let's learn more about animals and our environment.

Work with a friend and play some of the fun games in English. Then make a list of interesting information you find.

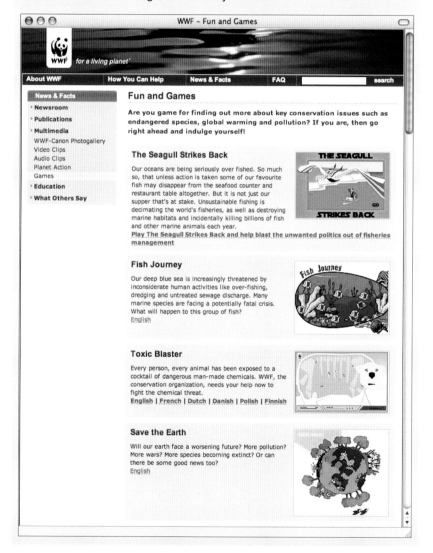

About WWF | How You Can Help | News & Facts | FAQ | search

News & Facts
- Newsroom
- Publications
- Multimedia
    - WWF-Canon Photogallery
    - Video Clips
    - Audio Clips
    - Planet Action
    - Games
- Education
- What Others Say

Fun and Games

Are you game for finding out more about key conservation issues such as endangered species, global warming and pollution? If you are, then go right ahead and indulge yourself!

The Seagull Strikes Back

Our oceans are being seriously over fished. So much so, that unless action is taken some of our favourite fish may disappear from the seafood counter and restaurant table altogether. But it is not just our supper that's at stake. Unsustainable fishing is decimating the world's fisheries, as well as destroying marine habitats and incidentally killing billions of fish and other marine animals each year.

Play The Seagull Strikes Back and help blast the unwanted politics out of fisheries management

Fish Journey

Our deep blue sea is increasingly threatened by inconsiderate human activities like over-fishing, dredging and untreated sewage discharge. Many marine species are facing a potentially fatal crisis. What will happen to this group of fish?
English

Toxic Blaster

Every person, every animal has been exposed to a cocktail of dangerous man-made chemicals. WWF, the conservation organization, needs your help now to fight the chemical threat.
English | French | Dutch | Danish | Polish | Finnish

Save the Earth

Will our earth face a worsening future? More pollution? More wars? More species becoming extinct? Or can there be some good news too?
English

BEFORE YOU READ

1 READING PICTURES

Look at the picture on pages 46 and 47 and answer these questions.

1 Who is on the grass?
2 Why is she there?
3 Describe her.
4 What is the man doing?
5 Why is Black Beauty standing in the meadow?

2 LISTENING

**Listen to Chapter Four and choose the correct answer (A, B or C).
There is an example at the beginning (0).**

0	Black Beauty is	A ✓	Lady Anne's favourite horse.
		B ☐	Lord Robert's favourite horse.
		C ☐	a nervous horse.
1	Lady Anne always brings Black Beauty	A ☐	some oats.
		B ☐	some sugar.
		C ☐	a carrot.
2	Some colts run by and	A ☐	Lizzie looks at them.
		B ☐	Lizzie is nervous.
		C ☐	Black Beauty follows them.
3	Black Beauty follows Lizzie and Lady Anne	A ☐	and then stops to drink at the river.
		B ☐	and falls to the ground.
		C ☐	because he wants to help his mistress.
4	Lady Anne falls off Lizzie	A ☐	when the horse jumps across a small river.
		B ☐	and dies.
		C ☐	and starts crying.
5	A young farmer returns from the village	A ☐	with Lizzie.
		B ☐	with a doctor.
		C ☐	with Lord Robert.
6	In the stable Black Beauty and Ginger	A ☐	talk about Lady Anne.
		B ☐	talk about Lizzie.
		C ☐	talk about Lord Robert.

CHAPTER FOUR

Lizzie

Lady Anne is a friend of Lord Wadsworth's family. She is young and beautiful, and a perfect rider. I am her favourite horse and I like carrying her. She is kind to me and always brings me a carrot. She often rides with her friend Lord Robert. He is a handsome young man with dark hair. He likes horses and often talks to me. He rides Lizzie, a young, nervous horse.

'What a lovely spring day!' says Lord Robert. 'Let's go riding, Lady Anne.'

'Alright,' she says, 'but I want to ride your horse today.'

'Lizzie's a good horse but she's too nervous for a lady,' says Lord Robert.

'What nonsense [1]!' says Lady Anne. 'Today I'm riding Lizzie and you're riding Black Beauty.'

Lord Robert is a good rider but I prefer Lady Anne because she is small and light. We gallop across the meadows and woods and have a wonderful time. Then we stop at Doctor Ashley's house.

1. **nonsense** : 胡說。

'I must give a letter to the doctor,' says Lord Robert.

'Lizzie and I can wait here with Black Beauty,' says Lady Anne.

After a few minutes some colts run by. Lizzie is nervous and she starts kicking. Lady Anne is afraid and suddenly Lizzie gallops away. I know Lizzie is dangerous, so I neigh [1] loudly and Lord Robert hears me. He runs to me and jumps on my back.

'Let's go, Beauty,' he cries. 'We must help Lady Anne.'

We follow Lizzie and Lady Anne. I gallop quickly because I want to help my mistress. Lizzie gallops up a hill and down into a valley. Lady Anne's green hat falls off and her long, brown hair flies in the wind. Then Lizzie jumps across a small river and Lady Anne falls off.

'Oh, no!' cries Lord Robert.

I jump across the river and see my poor mistress on the grass. Her face is white and her eyes are shut. She does not move or speak. Is she dead?

'Lady Anne, can you hear me?' asks Lord Robert.

But she does not answer.

1. **neigh** : 馬嘶。

A young farmer is walking by and says, 'The poor lady! Can I help her?'

'Yes,' says Lord Robert. 'Please go to the village and come back with the doctor. You can ride my horse, Beauty. He's very fast.'

The farmer gets on my back and I gallop to the village. He finds a doctor and we return to Lady Anne.

She is still on the grass and the doctor examines her carefully.

'Don't worry, she's not dead,' he says.

'But we must take her home right now and she must rest.'

I feel happy when I hear this because I like my young mistress. That evening in the stable Ginger and I talk about Lizzie.

Two days later Lord Robert comes to my stall and says, 'Lady Anne is better now and she wants to ride you soon. You are an intelligent [1] horse, Beauty, because you understand a lot of things.'

1. **intelligent** : 聰慧的。

UNDERSTANDING THE TEXT

1 COMPREHENSION CHECK
Are the following sentences true (T) or false (F)? Correct the false ones.

T   F

1 Lizzie is Lady Anne's favourite horse. ☐ ☐
2 Lord Robert doesn't like horses. ☐ ☐
3 Lord Robert stops at Doctor Ashley's house to give him a letter. ☐ ☐
4 Lizzie gallops away because she is nervous. ☐ ☐
5 Lord Robert and Black Beauty follow Lizzie and Lady Anne. ☐ ☐
6 Lady Anne falls off her horse and walks to the village. ☐ ☐

KET

2 CONVERSATIONS
Complete the five conversations. For questions 1-5 choose A, B or C. There is an example at the beginning (0).

0 How many horses are in the stable?
  A ☐ nothing
  B ☑ none
  C ☐ any

1 Can you ride a horse?
  A ☐ Yes, I can.
  B ☐ Yes, I do.
  C ☐ Yes, I am riding.

2 What time does the blacksmith open?
  A ☐ late
  B ☐ one hour
  C ☐ at half past nine

3 Where is the doctor's house?
  A ☐ Yes, there is.
  B ☐ I don't know.
  C ☐ into the town

4 Do you want to drink some water?
  A ☐ Yes, I want.
  B ☐ No, I'm not.
  C ☐ No, thank you.

5 Is your book interesting?
  A ☐ no very
  B ☐ Yes, it is.
  C ☐ a lot

3 ▶ CHARACTERS

Match each description (1-13) with a character (A-I). You can use some names more than once.

WHO...

1 ☐ is Lady Anne's friend?
2 ☐ is a young, nervous horse?
3 ☐ falls off her horse?
4 ☐ goes to the village to find a doctor?
5 ☐ is Lord Wadsworth's coachman?
6 ☐ is Black Beauty's mother?
7 ☐ is Jessie and Flora's favourite horse?
8 ☐ remembers cruel masters and the whip?
9 ☐ is a friend of Lord Wadsworth's family?
10 ☐ is handsome and has dark hair?
11 ☐ is a perfect rider?
12 ☐ wants the bearing rein?
13 ☐ wears a green hat?

A Merrylegs	D Lady Anne	G Duchess
B Lord Robert	E Ginger	H Mr York
C Lizzie	F Lady Wadsworth	I a young farmer

4 ▶ VOCABULARY

Find the words in the box that describe Lady Anne and Lord Robert and write them under their picture. Some words can be used more than once.

young	beautiful	perfect rider	handsome	dark hair
good rider	small	long, brown hair	light	likes horses	kind

Lady Anne

Lord Robert

....
....
....
....

....
....
....
....

THE DOCTOR EXAMINES HER CAREFULLY.

Carefully is an adverb（副詞）; it describes how the doctor examines her. We use adverbs to describe how we do something.

5 ADVERBS

Complete the sentences using the adverbs（副詞）in the box.

sadly	quietly	quickly	loudly	slowly	happily

1 Black Beauty neighs .... and Lord Robert hears him.
2 Jessie and Flora play .... in the field.
3 Ginger and Black Beauty say good-bye .... to their master.
4 Duchess is tired and walks ....
5 Black Beauty gallops .... because he wants to help his mistress.
6 Lady Anne speaks .... to Black Beauty.

T: GRADE 3
6 SPEAKING: FREE TIME
In Chapter Four Lady Anne is riding a horse with her friend. Use the questions below to talk about your free time.

1 Do you do any sports?
2 How often do you do it/them?
3 Where do you usually go?
4 Can you ride a horse?

BEFORE YOU READ

1 VOCABULARY
Match the words below with a picture.

A nails   B sharp stone   C knees

1️⃣   2️⃣   3️⃣

2 READING PICTURES
Look at the picture on page 53 and answer the following questions.

1 What is happening to the horse and the man?
2 Where are they?
3 What time of day is it?

CHAPTER FIVE

Reuben Smith

When Mr York goes to London, Reuben Smith becomes the coachman. He is a good, honest man and he understands horses. But he has one big problem: he drinks a lot and he is often drunk [1].

One morning he comes to my stall and says 'We're going to town on business, Beauty.' He puts my saddle on and we go.

When we arrive in town, Smith leaves me at a stable.

'My horse is hungry and thirsty,' says Smith to the stable boy. 'I'm coming back at four o'clock.'

The boy gives me oats and water, and looks at my horseshoes too.

'The nails in your front shoe are loose [2],' he says to me. 'You can't run with loose nails. I must tell Mr Smith.'

---

1. **drunk** : 喝醉的。
2. **loose** : 鬆動的。此處指不在其位。

But Smith does not come at four o'clock and he does not come at five o'clock. The boy is worried and I am, too.

At nine o'clock in the evening Smith comes back. He is angry and his voice is loud. He cannot walk well.

'The front shoe of your horse has loose nails, sir,' says the boy. 'It's dangerous to ride a horse with loose nails.'

Smith looks at him and shouts, 'It's late! I'm going home.'

It is a dark night and the moon is behind the clouds.

'Come on, Beauty. Gallop!' he cries and hits me with his whip. I gallop fast but my front shoe is loose. I feel the whip again.

'Gallop, Beauty!' cries Smith again.

At the bridge my front shoe falls off. My foot hurts a lot. There are a lot of sharp stones on the road. I try to gallop but I can't. At last I fall heavily on my knees and Smith falls off. I get up slowly and look at Smith. He is not moving. What can I do?

Soon I hear Ginger coming. I neigh loudly and she answers. Then I hear men's voices and they stop in front of Smith.

'It's Reuben,' says one man. 'He's dead.'

'Dead?' says another man.

'Yes,' says the first man sadly. 'Poor Reuben Smith. Look at his head!'

Then the man looks at me. 'Look at this poor horse. It's Black Beauty. His knees are badly hurt.'

The men slowly take me back to the stable, but I cannot sleep. The next day the vet and the blacksmith come to see me.

'This horse must rest for a few months,' says the vet.

So now I stay in the green meadow with its sweet grass. But I am worried about the future because my knees are not perfect.

After a month Ginger comes to the meadow too, because she is very tired. I like talking to my old friend under the apple tree.

One summer day Lord Wadsworth and York come to the meadow. They look at my knees.

'I'm sorry, York, but I must sell Black Beauty,' says the lord. 'His knees are not perfect anymore. I can't keep a horse with those knees in my stables. I'm very sorry because I like Beauty. He's a wonderful horse, but his knees...'

When they go away Ginger says sadly, 'You're the only friend I've got and soon you must leave. What a difficult [1] life.'

I look at her and say, 'Ginger, you're my true friend.'

---

1. **difficult**：困難的。

The lord sells me to the town livery stables [1]. It is not a nice place. Anyone can hire [2] a horse and carriage at the livery stables. Most of the drivers are bad and know nothing about horses. And of course they know nothing about driving a carriage. They make a lot of mistakes [3] and then get angry with the horse and use the whip.

In the evening I cannot talk about my day because I do not know the other horses. I am very lonely and think about Ginger.

1. **livery stables**：車馬出租所。
2. **hire**：租用。
3. **make a lot of mistakes**：犯許多錯誤。

UNDERSTANDING THE TEXT

KET

① COMPREHENSION CHECK

Choose the correct answer (A, B or C). There is an example at the beginning (0).

0 Reuben Smith's big problem is that he

A ☐ is a bad man.

B ☐ is dishonest.

C ☑ drinks a lot.

1 Reuben Smith leaves Black Beauty

A ☐ at a stable.

B ☐ in a green meadow.

C ☐ in a forest.

2 When the stable boy looks at Black Beauty's horseshoe, he understands that

A ☐ it is broken.

B ☐ the nails are loose.

C ☐ it is too small.

3 Reuben Smith comes to the stable

A ☐ at nine o'clock in the evening.

B ☐ at four o'clock in the afternoon.

C ☐ early the next day.

4 Black Beauty falls on his knees because

A ☐ it is raining.

B ☐ he is galloping too fast.

C ☐ his front shoe falls off.

5 When Reuben Smith falls, he hurts

A ☐ his knees.

B ☐ his head and dies.

C ☐ his foot.

6 Lord Wadsworth sells Black Beauty to the livery stables because

A ☐ he is old.

B ☐ he cannot gallop.

C ☐ his knees are not perfect anymore.

2 LISTENING

Listen to the conversation between Reuben Smith and the stable boy. Choose the correct answer (A, B or C). There is an example at the beginning (0).

0 What time does the stable close?

A

B ✓

C

1 How much do oats and water cost?

A

B

C

2 What does Reuben buy at the stable?

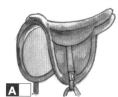
A

B

C

3 Where can Reuben buy a blanket for his horse?

A

B

C

4 Where is the town inn?

A

B

C

③ CHARACTERS

Who says what? Match the sentences (1-8) with a character (A-F). You can use one character more than once.

1 ☐ 'His knees are badly hurt.'
2 ☐ 'You can't run with loose nails.'
3 ☐ 'I can't keep a horse with those knees in my stables.'
4 ☐ 'You're the only friend I've got.'
5 ☐ 'Come on, Beauty. Gallop!'
6 ☐ 'This horse must rest for a few months.'
7 ☐ 'We're going to town on business, Beauty.'
8 ☐ 'My horse is hungry and thirsty.'

A Reuben Smith   C vet   E one man
B stable boy   D Lord Wadsworth F Ginger

BEFORE YOU READ

① VOCABULARY

Match the pictures to the words below.

A cab stand   B cart   C bones   D prison

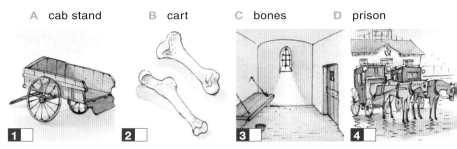

1 ☐   2 ☐   3 ☐   4 ☐

② READING PICTURES

Look at the pictures on pages 60 and 61 and answer these questions.

1 What is this place?
2 What are the horses doing there?
3 What are the men saying?

Look at the picture on page 63 and answer these questions.

1 Are the horses in a village or a city?
2 What are they doing?
3 One of the two horses in not happy. Why?

CHAPTER SIX

A London Cab [1] Horse

After a year at the livery stables the master takes me to a horse fair. He wants to sell me. A horse fair is an interesting place. Some of the horses at the fair are young and handsome, but most of them are old and tired. Their eyes are sad and they are thin and hungry.

I am still a strong horse but my knees are not perfect anymore. People come to look at me, and they like me. But when they see my knees they go away.

At the end of the day a tall, thin man comes and looks at me. Then he talks to my master.

'I'm looking for a gentle horse,' he says. 'I want to ride him in the fresh air every morning.'

'This black horse is perfect,' says my master. 'He's very gentle.'

My new master is Mr Barry and he lives in Bath. He knows

1. **Cab**：載人小馬車。

59

nothing about horses but he is a kind man. He buys a lot of food but the stable boy steals [1] it and takes it home. He is dishonest and lazy. He never cleans my feet or my stall. Mr Barry knows nothing about this.

One day Mr Barry's friend says, 'Your horse is very thin. What's the matter with him?'

'I don't know,' says Mr Barry. 'I always buy a lot of food for him.'

'Go and see what's happening in the stable,' says his friend.

1. **steals** : 偷。

My master discovers that the stable boy steals my food and my stall is very dirty. He is angry and calls the police. They take the stable boy to prison for two months.

Then Mr Barry comes to my stall and looks at me sadly. 'I'm sorry, Beauty,' he says, 'I must sell you at the next horse fair. I'm not lucky with horses.'

I am sorry too because I do not like changing masters.

At the next horse fair a short man with kind grey eyes comes to look at me. He pats my neck gently and smiles.

'I like this horse,' he says to the man. 'I can pay twenty-four pounds for him.'

'Very well, the horse is yours,' says the man.

My new master is a cab driver and lives in London.

His name is Jerry Barker and his wife's name is Polly. They have got two children, Dolly and Harry. They are a very happy family and they like me.

Captain is Jerry's other horse. He is a big, white horse and he seems friendly.

Our cab stand is in the centre of London and there are many horses.

Jerry is an excellent driver, and he never uses the whip or the bearing rein. Our stable is clean and we are never hungry. I am lucky to have a kind master.

Sunday is the best day because I can rest all day and talk to Captain. He is an old military horse [1] and tells me exciting stories about different wars.

The life of a cab horse is difficult. London is a big city with a lot of noise, people, carriages and cabs. The weather is often wet and cold. At the end of the day I am very tired and my knees hurt. Captain has the same problem.

In the winter Dolly often brings her father a hot lunch. He eats it at the cab stand. Jerry's life is difficult too.

One day our cab is waiting outside a park. Another cab stops next to us. An old, tired brown horse is pulling the cab. The poor horse has a long, thin neck and her eyes are almost shut. I can see her bones through her dirty coat. She looks at me with her sad eyes and says, 'Is that you, Black Beauty?'

'Ginger! My old friend,' I answer. 'Yes, it's me, Black Beauty.'

'It's good to see you,' says Ginger. 'I feel terrible. I am old, weak [2], hungry and ill. I can't run or gallop anymore. I must pull this heavy cab for my cruel master and I eat very little. I work all week and never have a day of rest. Every bone in my old body hurts.'

'How terrible!' I put my nose near hers. 'Dear Ginger, I'm very sorry.'

A week later I see a cart [3] with a dead horse in it – it is Ginger. I feel very sad when I see her body in the cart.

Why are people cruel to animals? They do not understand us. We only want some love and kindness.

1. **military horse**：戰馬。
2. **weak**：虛弱。
3. **cart**：手推車。

UNDERSTANDING THE TEXT

 **SUMMARY**

Choose a word from the box to complete each space.

ill	London	body	Jerry Barker	cruel	horse fair
cab	tired	police	difficult	heavy	good
	dishonest	prison	home		

The master wants to sell Black Beauty at the (1) ....
Mr Barry is looking for a gentle horse and buys Beauty.

He lives in Bath and knows nothing about horses. He is a
(2) .... man but his stable boy is lazy and (3) ....
He steals the horse's food and takes it (4) .... When Mr Barry
discovers this he calls the (5) .... and the stable boy goes to
(6) .... for two months.

Black Beauty's next master is (7) .... He is a cab driver in
(8) .... and a kind master. He never uses the whip or the
bearing rein.

The life of a cab horse is (9) .... and Black Beauty is very
(10) .... at the end of the day.

One day he sees Ginger in another (11) .... She is
(12) .... and weak and has a (13) .... master.
She must pull a (14) .... cab all week. She can't run or
gallop anymore. After a week Black Beauty sees Ginger's dead
(15) .... in a cart and he is very sad.

KEY

 VOCABULARY

**Read the definitions. What is the word for each one? The first letter is
already there. There is one space for each letter in the word. There is
an example at the beginning (0).**

0	horses sleep here at night	s t a b l e
1	you can buy a horse here	f _ _ _
2	the sound a horse makes	n _ _ _ _
3	an animal doctor	v _ _
4	not alive	d _ _ _
5	to clean and brush an animal	g _ _ _ _

③ CHARACTERS

Do you remember the horses in the story? Choose the adjectives（形容詞）or expressions（措辭）that describe them and write them under their pictures. Some words can be used more than once.

black   old   grey   friendly   brown   fast   white   handsome
quiet   kicks and bites   young   big   happy   wise   nervous
military horse   comes from a good family   tells stories about the war

Duchess

....
....
....
....

Merrylegs

....
....
....
....

Ginger

....
....
....
....

Max

....
....
....
....

Lizzie

....
....
....
....

Captain

....
....
....
....

Black Beauty

....
....
....
....

Now write a sentence about your favourite horse in the story and say why you like him/her.

....

Horses

Horses are beautiful animals. They are intelligent and friendly. And they learn quickly too. Their favourite foods are oats, carrots and apples. They do not eat meat.

Horses love conversation! You can talk to a horse and he listens to you happily.

There are three types of horses: light, heavy and ponies. Each kind of horse has a lot of breeds. Breeds are groups of horses with different colours and sizes.

1 *Light horses* – they have small bones and thin legs, and they weigh about 650 kilograms.

Saddle horses are light horses. People use them for riding. Some important breeds of saddle horses are Thoroughbred horses, American Saddle horses and Arabian Stallions **1**.

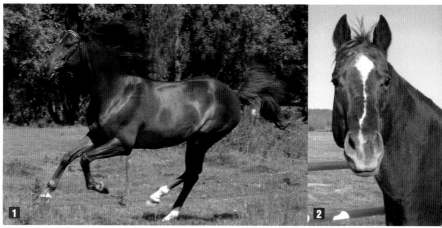

Quarter horses **2** – they are fast, strong and intelligent. They work well with other animals.

Lipizzaner horses – they are beautiful show horses. They have a white coat and strong legs. These horses are part of the Spanish Riding School in Vienna, Austria. It is a very famous riding school. You can visit it and watch the Lipizzaner horses dance to music!

2 *Heavy horses* – they have big bones and big legs, and they weigh around 1,300 kilograms.

Draft horses are very tall, heavy and strong. People use them for heavy work and in shows. Some important breeds of draft horses are Clydesdale horses **3**, Shire horses and Percheron horses **4**.

3 *Ponies* – they are small, short horses and they weigh around 400 kilograms.

Ponies are gentle. They are good horses for young riders. They are strong, clever animals. Some important breeds of ponies are Shetland ponies **5**, Welsh ponies and Dartmoor ponies **6**.

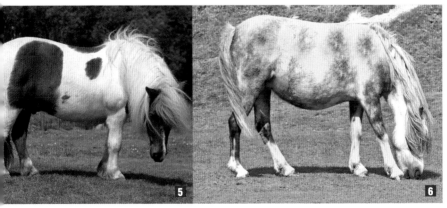

Horses at work

Today cars, buses, trains and airplanes take people everywhere. But horses are still part of our lives. We ride horses for fun and sport. We watch them perform at the circus. People go to the horse races and watch their favourite horse. Cowboys ride bucking broncos [1] at rodeos [2] in the United States.

Policemen and policewomen ride horses in big cities like New York City. Cowboys in North American ranches [3] ride quarter horses when they work with cattle.

A ride in a horse and carriage is a big tourist attraction in some towns and cities.

In poor countries people use horses to work on farms and to travel. In some north European countries horses and ponies pull sleighs [4] in the snow.

Horses and carriages waiting for tourists.

1. **bucking broncos**：野馬。
2. **rodeos**：騎術表演。
3. **ranches**：牧場。
4. **sleighs**：雪橇。

① COMPREHENSION CHECK

Are these questions true (T) or false (F)? Correct the false ones.

		T	F
1	Horses like eating oats and meat.	☐	☐
2	There are three types of horses.	☐	☐
3	Saddle horses are small, short horses.	☐	☐
4	Cowboys use quarter horses for ranch work.	☐	☐
5	Arabian Stallions are draft horses.	☐	☐
6	Lipizzaner horses are white and beautiful.	☐	☐
7	Draft horses are big and weigh around 1,300 kilograms.	☐	☐
8	Ponies are good horses for young riders.	☐	☐
9	People use saddle horses for riding.	☐	☐
10	Lipizzaner horses are heavy horses.	☐	☐
11	Some people use horses to work on farms.	☐	☐
12	Policemen cannot ride horses in big cities.	☐	☐

② What other jobs do horses do today? Compare your answers with a friend.

PROJECT ON THE WEB

LET'S VISIT THE FAMOUS SPANISH RIDING SCHOOL IN VIENNA, AUSTRIA!

Connect to the Internet and go to www.blackcat-cideb.com or www.cideb.it. Insert the title or part of the title of the book into our search engine. Open the page for *Black Beauty*. Click on the Internet project link.

Click on *English*, then on *Visitor Information*, then on *Famous School Stallions*.

Look at the story of the famous horse **Siglavy Mantua** I and fill in the information:

Born

     When: ....

     Where: ....

Where he lives and works: ....

Who his rider is: ....

BEFORE YOU READ

1 **WHAT HAPPENS NEXT?**
Tick the answer you think is correct.

A ☐ Black Beauty stays with Jerry Barker.
B ☐ Jerry sells him to a good master.
C ☐ Jerry sells him to a cruel master.

2 **READING PICTURES**
Look at the picture on page 73 and answer these questions.

1 How does Black Beauty look?
2 What is the little girl saying to the man?
3 What is the cab driver doing?

KET

3 **LISTENING**
Listen to the first part of Chapter Seven and choose the correct answer (A, B or C).

1 On New Year's Eve Jerry and Black Beauty
   A ☐ stay at home.
   B ☐ take two gentlemen to a restaurant.
   C ☐ take two gentlemen to a party.

2 Jerry becomes very ill because
   A ☐ he waits out in the cold.
   B ☐ he eats too much on New Year's Eve.
   C ☐ he falls off the cab.

3 Black Beauty's new master
   A ☐ is called Harry.
   B ☐ drives an old cab.
   C ☐ is a kind old man.

4 Black Beauty works
   A ☐ very little and eats a lot.
   B ☐ twelve hours a day and eats little.
   C ☐ on a big farm with other horses.

5 At the railway station there is a family
   A ☐ with five children.
   B ☐ with a lot of big boxes.
   C ☐ with a lot of heavy luggage.

CHAPTER SEVEN

My Last Home

Christmas and New Year's Eve are happy times for some people, but not for cab drivers and their horses. During that time we work hard and stay out late. Often we must wait for hours in the rain or snow while people are at parties.

On New Year's Eve Jerry and I take two gentlemen to a party in a big house.

'Come back for us at eleven o'clock and don't be late,' says one of the gentlemen.

At eleven o'clock we are in front of the big house but the gentlemen are not there. It is a very cold night and it is snowing.

'The church bell says it's midnight,' says Jerry, 'but the gentlemen are not here.'

We continue to wait in the cold.

Black Beauty

At a quarter past one the door of the big house opens and the two gentlemen come out. They do not say a word to Jerry and we take them home.

When we get home Jerry cannot speak and he coughs [1] a lot. He dries me and puts a warm blanket on my back.

The next morning Harry comes to give me oats and water. He pats my neck gently and says, 'My father is very ill. He can't drive his cab anymore. He must find another job. We must sell you to another cab driver. I'm very sorry, dear old friend.'

Dolly comes and kisses me, then she starts crying. 'Goodbye, old friend.'

I am very sad to leave Jerry and his family.

My new master is Nicholas Skinner. He has black eyes and black hair, and a loud voice. He drives an old cab in a bad part of London. He often whips my back and my head. He is a cruel master, but I always do my best.

I eat little and work twelve hours a day, seven days a week. There is no time to rest or to talk to other horses. My life is very unhappy.

One morning we go to the railway station and pick up a lady, a man, a young girl and a little boy. They have a lot of heavy luggage [2]. Skinner puts all the luggage in the cab. The young girl comes and looks at me.

'Father,' she says, 'this poor horse can't take us and all our luggage. He is weak and thin. Please come and look at him.'

'What nonsense!' says the man. 'Get in the cab at once and be quiet.'

I start to pull the heavy cab to Ludgate Hill. Then I try to climb

---

1. **coughs** : 咳嗽。

2. **luggage** : 行李。

the hill but I feel weak. Suddenly I fall to the ground. I try to get up but I cannot.

'Oh, the poor horse!' cries the young girl. 'We are cruel.'

A young man throws some cold water on my head, and I slowly get up.

Skinner takes me back to the stables and says, 'You're working very hard. Rest for a week and then I must sell you at the horse fair. You're not a good horse for my cab.'

The horses at the fair are old and tired. And the people are not rich gentlemen, they are farmers. A farmer and his grandson stop in front of me.

'Look at this horse, William,' says the farmer. 'He is tired and thin, but he is handsome. He comes from a good family. Look at his neck and ears.'

The young boy pats my face and I put my nose in his hand.

'Look, grandfather, he likes me,' says William.

'Do you like him?' asks the grandfather.

'Yes, I like him a lot,' says the young boy happily. The grandfather looks at my teeth and my legs.

'Well, I'm buying him for you, William,' says the grandfather. 'You must look after him. You must feed him and groom him every day. You can make him feel better. He is your responsibility.' [1]

'Oh, thank you, grandfather!' says William, kissing him. 'I promise [2] to look after him.'

William and Mr Turner take me to their stables. I have a big, clean stall with lots of oats and fresh water. There is a small meadow outside where I can eat grass and enjoy the sun. Young William is a perfect master.

1. **He is your responsibility** : 照顧牠是你的職責。
2. **promise** : 答應。

'Now you must rest, Beauty,' says William. 'Soon you can run in the meadow with the other horses.'

Mr Turner works on the farm and sometimes he comes to see me. He looks at my legs and my teeth. Then he talks to me and gives me some sugar.

'Black Beauty is feeling better,' says Mr Turner to William. 'His legs and knees are strong now. You're doing a good job with this horse.'

William smiles and says, 'Thank you, grandfather. I love Black Beauty.'

'I do too,' says Mr Turner. 'He's a wonderful horse.'

The Blomefield sisters are friends of Mr Turner, and they are looking for a good horse.

'Black Beauty is feeling fine now,' says Mr Turner. 'Let's take him to the Blomefield sisters and see what they say.'

'Yes grandfather,' says William. 'What a good idea!'

One summer day William and Mr Turner take me to visit their friends.

Ellen Blomefield and her two sisters are happy when they see me.

'This horse has a good face and he's very handsome,' says Ellen. 'I like him. Can I try him for a week?'

'Yes, of course,' says Mr Turner happily.

A stable boy takes me to a big stable and starts grooming me.

Every morning he comes to my stall and pats me and talks to me.

'Good morning, Beauty,' he says. 'What a lovely day! You can go to the meadow today.'

He grooms me and gives me an apple. Then he takes me to the meadow.

I like the tall trees and the beautiful flowers. I feel better every day.

'This is the same star Black Beauty has,' says the young man, looking at the white star on my face. 'And this is the same white foot too.' He looks at my back and sees a little white spot [1].

'Oh, this is Black Beauty!' he cries. 'Black Beauty, do you remember me? I'm Joe Green the stable boy at Mr Gordon's.'

I put my nose in his hand. Yes, it is Joe Green. He is very happy and tells the Blomefield sisters about me. They are happy too and they want to keep me forever [2].

Now I am part of the Blomefield family. Ellen rides me almost every day and I am her favourite horse. Sometimes I take her sisters to town in the carriage. My good friends Mr Turner and William often come to visit me.

I am finally happy in this wonderful home, because everyone loves me and I love them.

1. **spot** : 斑點。   2. **forever** : 永遠。

UNDERSTANDING THE TEXT

1 COMPREHENSION CHECK

Read Chapter Seven and choose the correct answer (A, B or C). There is an example at the beginning (0).

0 On New Year's Eve Jerry becomes ill

A ☐ but he continues working.

B ☐ and he must go to a warm country.

C ☑ and he cannot drive his cab anymore.

1 Jerry sells Black Beauty to

A ☐ a cab driver called Nicholas Skinner.

B ☐ a cart driver called Harry.

C ☐ two rich gentlemen.

2 One day Black Beauty pulls the cab

A ☐ across London Bridge.

B ☐ down Ludgate Hill.

C ☐ up Ludgate Hill.

3 Black Beauty falls to the ground and cannot get up because

A ☐ he is hungry and thirsty.

B ☐ the cab is too heavy.

C ☐ it is raining.

4 Mr Turner is a farmer and

A ☐ he buys Black Beauty for his grandson.

B ☐ he buys Black Beauty for Ellen Blomefield.

C ☐ Black Beauty must work on his farm.

5 Joe Green remembers Black Beauty's white star and white foot

A ☐ and he becomes Black Beauty's new master.

B ☐ and he tells the Blomefield sisters.

C ☐ but he doesn't tell anyone.

6 Ellen Blomefield and her sisters

A ☐ like Black Beauty and keep him forever.

B ☐ sell Black Beauty to Joe Green.

C ☐ don't want a horse with bad knees.

2 PREPOSITIONS

Complete the sentences with the prepositions（介詞）in the box.

with	under	on	for	about	at	in (x 2)	up	outside

1 Jerry's cab is waiting .... the park.

2 The man .... black hair has a loud voice.

3 The horses are resting .... the stable.

4 Mr Barry knows nothing .... the lazy stable boy.

5 Ginger pulls a heavy cab .... her master.

6 Black Beauty is standing .... the tree.

7 Mr Turner visits the Blomefield sisters .... Saturday afternoon.

8 William has dinner .... six o'clock.

9 Black Beauty is climbing .... the hill.

10 Jerry and Black Beauty are waiting .... the cold rain.

KEY

3 FILL IN THE GAPS

Complete these letters. Write one word for each space (1-10). There is an example at the beginning (0).

Dear Pamela,

I have (0) ......*a*........ new horse. (1) .... name is Black Beauty. He is a beautiful black horse (2) .... a white star on his forehead.

I ride (3) .... almost every day. He (4) .... a gentle horse and never bites or kicks. He takes my sisters to town on Sundays.

Come (5) .... see Black Beauty one day.

Ellen

Dear Ellen,

I am glad to hear about your new horse, Black Beauty.

My brother (6) .... I have a new dog. Her name is Diane and she is brown and white and has long ears. My brother goes hunting (7) .... her. She is great fun and likes playing with me.

I can come and visit (8) .... and (9) .... sisters on Wednesday afternoon (10) .... two o'clock.

Pamela

4 LISTENING

Listen to the conversation between Ellen Blomefield and Mr Turner. Then choose the correct answer (A, B or C). There is an example at the beginning (0).

0 Where does Ellen meet Mr Turner?

A ☐

B ☑

C ☐

1 What is she buying?

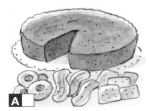

A ☐

B ☐

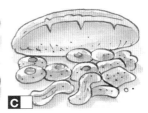

C ☐

2 How old is Black Beauty?

6
A ☐

15
B ☐

5
C ☐

3 When can Mr Turner bring the horse to Ellen's house?

6
Tuesday
A ☐

25
Thursday
B ☐

10
Saturday
C ☐

4 Where does Ellen live?

A☐   B☐   C☐

5 How much does the horse cost?

  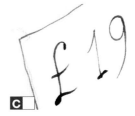

A☐   B☐   C☐

5 **VOCABULARY**
Complete the crossword.

Across

2 horses like eating them

4 in the country horses run here

6

8

10 horses live here

11 the colour of grass

12 very unkind

Down

1

3 Black Beauty's mother

5 he looks after horses

7

9 horses pull this

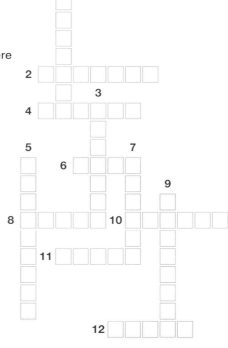

EXIT TEST 1

1 COMPREHENSION CHECK

Are these sentences 'Right' (A) or 'Wrong' (B). If there is not enough information to answer 'Right' (A) or 'Wrong' (B), choose 'Doesn't say' (C).

1   Black Beauty comes from a family of famous horses.
   A Right   B Wrong   C Doesn't say

2   Black Beauty's first home is at Mr Gordon's.
   A Right   B Wrong   C Doesn't say

3   Ginger is Jessie and Flora's favourite horse.
   A Right   B Wrong   C Doesn't say

4   Black Beauty doesn't cross the bridge because he is afraid.
   A Right   B Wrong   C Doesn't say

5   Mrs Gordon is fifty years old and is very ill.
   A Right   B Wrong   C Doesn't say

6   Black Beauty and Ginger must wear the bearing rein with Lady Wadsworth.
   A Right   B Wrong   C Doesn't say

7   Lady Anne doesn't want to ride Lizzie because she is a nervous horse.
   A Right   B Wrong   C Doesn't say

8   Black Beauty falls on his knees because his foot is hurt.
   A Right   B Wrong   C Doesn't say

9   Lord Wadsworth sells Black Beauty and Ginger to the livery stables.
   A Right   B Wrong   C Doesn't say

10 Jerry Barker and his family live in a small white house near Ludgate Hill.
   A Right   B Wrong   C Doesn't say

11 Jerry cannot drive a cab anymore so he sells Black Beauty to Nicholas Skinner.
   A Right   B Wrong   C Doesn't say

12 Black Beauty cannot climb the hill and falls to the ground.
   A Right   B Wrong   C Doesn't say

13 The Blomefield sisters are friends of Mr Turner and they keep Black Beauty forever.
   A Right   B Wrong   C Doesn't say

SCORE

② CHARACTERS

Match the descriptions (1-12) to the characters (A-L).

WHO...

1 ☐ promises to look after Black Beauty?
2 ☐ puts heavy metal shoes on horses?
3 ☐ is a farmer?
4 ☐ goes to visit the Duchess of Barstow?
5 ☐ has a horse with a bad leg?
6 ☐ is Black Beauty's best friend?
7 ☐ drinks a lot?
8 ☐ is Lizzie's master?
9 ☐ whips Black Beauty's back and head?
10 ☐ wants to try Black Beauty for a week?
11 ☐ tells the Blomefield sisters about Black Beauty?
12 ☐ has a white star on his forehead?

A Lady Wadsworth
B Ginger
C Reuben Smith
D Joe Green
E Ellen Blomefield
F The blacksmith

G Lord Robert
H William
I Dr White
J Black Beauty
K Mr Turner
L Nicholas Skinner

SCORE

EXIT TEST 2

1 CONTEXT
Answer the following questions.

1   What is the author's name?
2   Is the author American or British?
3   What is the RSPCA and what does it do?
4   How many types of horses are there?
5   Name three breeds of horses.
6   What do horses like to eat?
7   What is the Spanish Riding School?

2 COMPREHENSION CHECK
Are the following sentences true (T) or false (F)? Correct the false ones.

		T	F
1	When Black Beauty is four years old Mr Gordon comes to look at him.	☐	☐
2	Black Beauty does not like carrying his master.	☐	☐
3	Black Beauty and Ginger do not like the bearing rein.	☐	☐
4	Lizzie is Lady Anne's favourite horse.	☐	☐
5	Lord Wadsworth sells Black Beauty because his knees are not perfect.	☐	☐
6	Mr Barry is a cruel master.	☐	☐
7	Jerry Barker is a London cab driver.	☐	☐
8	Black Beauty has an unhappy life with Nicholas Skinner.	☐	☐
9	William Turner looks after Black Beauty.	☐	☐
10	Ellen Blomefield and her sisters do not want a horse with bad knees.	☐	☐

3 VOCABULARY
Match the opposites.

1   light
2   inside
3   cruel
4   fast
5   weak
6   fat

7 tall
8 old
9 wet
A strong
B slow
C kind
D outside
E heavy
F dry
G young
H short
I thin

4 PREPOSITIONS
Complete the sentences with the prepositions in the box.

about	with	up	across	in	at	on	under	for

1 The woman .... the green hat is Lady Anne.
2 Jerry Barker and Black Beauty wait .... the rain.
3 Ellen and her sisters have dinner .... half past six.
4 Black Beauty does not want to go .... the bridge.
5 Mr Barry is kind but he knows nothing .... horses.
6 The oats and the water are .... Ginger.
7 Mr Gordon is going to London .... Wednesday.
8 Black Beauty cannot climb .... Ludgate Hill.
9 Max and Lizzie are resting .... the apple tree.

5 WRITING
Write answers to the following questions.

1 Do you like the story? Why? Why not?

    ....

2 Who is your favourite character?

    ....

3 What is your favourite part of the story?

    ....

Black Beauty

KEY TO
THE EXERCISES
AND EXIT TESTS

KEY TO THE EXERCISES

A. Sewell

Let's meet Anna Sewell

Page 10 – exercise 1

A9 **B**1 **C**7 **D**17 **E**10 **F**6 **G**4 **H**5
I13 **J**16 **K**12 **L**14 **M**15 **N**11 **O**2
P8 **Q**3

Page 12 – exercise 2

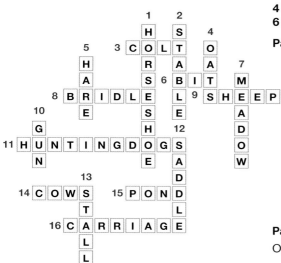

Chapter ONE

Page 19 – exercise 1

1C **2**A **3**C **4**B **5**B **6**A **7**B **8**C **9**A
10A **11**A **12**B

Page 20 – exercise 2

1 carriage **2** colt **3** saddle
4 bridle, bit **5** blacksmith, horseshoes
6 stable **7** stall

Page 20 – exercise 3

Page 20 – exercise 4

Open answer

Page 21 – exercise 5

Countable: carrot, apple, egg, orange, banana, cow, horseshoe, cake
Uncountable: milk, rain, money, butter, meat, bread, music, grass

Page 21 – exercise 1

1 night
2 it's raining
3 a man
4 he is telling them to go back because the bridge is broken
5 the master and John
6 because he knows something is wrong

Page 22 – exercise 2

1 bell **2** blanket **3** bridge
4 coachman **5** gallop **6** whip

Page 22 – exercise 3

1T **2**F **3**T **4**T **5**F **6**T **7**F **8**T

Chapter TWO

Page 29 – exercise 1

1C **2**B **3**C **4**A **5**C **6**B

Page 30 – exercise 2

1 His **2** is **3** has **4** on **5** from **6** and
7 in **8** am **9** with **10** hope

Page 30 – exercise 3

1 boat **2** sleep **3** month **4** neighbour
5 bridge

1 month **2** sleep **3** bridge **4** boat
5 neighbour

Page 30 – exercise 4

Friendly, kind, good, understanding, good rider, coachman

Page 31 – exercise 5

1 Black Beauty **2** black **3** white star
4 stable **5** Mr Gordon **6** John Manly
7 oats **8** Ginger **9** Merrylegs

Page 31 – exercise 6

1D **2**F **3**H **4**G **5**B

Page 32 – exercise 1

(Picture on pages 34-35)
1 He is looking at Black Beauty.
2 Black Beauty is in his stall.

(Picture on pages 36-37)
1 The horses are jumping up and Ginger is kicking.
2 He is trying to pull her down.
3 The lady is screaming because she is afraid.
4 It is a very big and beautiful house.

Page 32 – exercise 2

1B **2**A **3**C **4**B **5**A

Chapter THREE

Page 38 – exercise 1

1C **2**A **3**A **4**B **5**C **6**B **7**A **8**C **9**A
10C **11**B **12**A

Page 39 – exercise 2

1F **2**D **3**A **4**G **5**B **6**H **7**E **8**C

Page 39 – exercise 3

1 stable **2** colt **3** oats **4** saddle
5 gun **6** blanket **7** pat **8** vet **9** cruel

Page 40 – exercise 4

1D **2**C **3**G **4**F **5**E

The Royal Society for the Prevention of Cruelty to Animals

Page 42 – exercise 1

1 F – Richard Martin opens the Society for the Prevention of Cruelty to Animals.
2 T
3 F – Today there are more than 400 inspectors in the RSPCA.
4 T
5 T

Page 44 – exercise 1

1 A lady is on the grass.
2 She is not feeling well.
3 She is young and has got long brown hair and a long dress.
4 He is trying to help her.
5 He is waiting for the man and the lady.

Page 44 – exercise 2

1C **2**B **3**C **4**A **5**B **6**B

Chapter FOUR

Page 48 – exercise 1

1 F – Black Beauty is her favourite horse.
2 F – He likes horses.
3 T
4 T
5 T
6 F – Lady Anne falls off her horse and stays on the grass.

Page 48 – exercise 2

1A **2**C **3**B **4**C **5**B

Page 49 – exercise 3

1B **2**C **3**D **4**I **5**H **6**G **7**A **8**E **9**D
10B **11**D **12**F **13**D

Page 49 – exercise 4

Lady Anne: young, beautiful, perfect rider, small, long, brown hair, light, likes horses, kind
Lord Robert: young, handsome, dark hair, good rider, likes horses, kind

Page 50 – exercise 5

1 loudly **2** happily **3** sadly **4** slowly
5 quickly **6** quietly

Page 50 – exercise 6

Open answer

Page 50 – exercise 1

1C **2**A **3**B

Page 50 – exercise 2

1 The horse and the man are both falling.
2 They are on a small road in the forest.
3 It is night.

Chapter FIVE

Page 56 – exercise 1

1A **2**B **3**A **4**C **5**B **6**C

Page 57 – exercise 2

1B **2**B **3**A **4**C

Recording script
Reuben: Good Morning! Is this Jones's Stables?
Boy: Yes, sir. Can I help you?
Reuben: I'm in town on business today. Can I leave my horse here?
Boy: Yes, of course,
Reuben: What time do you close?
Boy: We close at 10 p.m.
Reuben: Good. I'm coming back at 4 p.m. My horse is hungry and thirsty. How much do oats and water cost?
Boy: Four pence, sir.
Reuben: I want to buy some new reins too.
Boy: We have brown and black reins.
Reuben: Good, I want two black reins. Do you sell blankets too?
Boy: No, we don't, sir.
Reuben: Where can I buy a blanket for my horse?
Boy: At Mr Smith's shop near the town inn.
Reuben: Where's the town inn?
Boy: It's behind the church.
Reuben: Thank you.

Page 58 – exercise 3

1E **2**B **3**D **4**F **5**A **6**C **7**A **8**A

Page 58 – exercise 1

1B **2**C **3**D **4**A

Page 58 – exercise 2

(Picture on pages 60-61)
1 It is a horse fair
2 They are waiting for someone to buy them.
3 They are talking about the horses.

(Picture on page 63)
1 They are in a city.
2 They are waiting at a cab stand.
3 The horse is not happy because she is tired, cold, hungry and thin.

Chapter SIX

Page 64 – exercise 1

1 horse fair 2 good 3 dishonest
4 home 5 police 6 prison
7 Jerry Barker 8 London 9 difficult
10 tired 11 cab 12 ill 13 cruel
14 heavy 15 body

Page 64 – exercise 2

1 fair 2 neigh 3 vet 4 dead 5 groom

Page 65 – exercise 3

Duchess: black, old, wise, comes from a good family
Merrylegs: friendly, happy
Ginger: brown, fast, kicks and bites
Max: grey, quiet
Lizzie: fast, nervous
Captain: old, white, military horse, tells stories about the war
Black Beauty: black, friendly, fast, handsome, young, happy, comes from a good family

Horses

Page 69 – exercise 1

1 F – Horses like oats but they do not eat meat.
2 T
3 F – Saddle horses are light horses.
4 T
5 F – Arabian Stallions are light horses.
6 T
7 T
8 T
9 T
10 F – Lippizzaner horses are light horses.
11 T
12 F – Policemen and policewomen ride horses in big cities.

Page 69 – exercise 2

Open answer

Page 70 – exercise 1

Open answer

Page 70 – exercise 2

1 Black Beauty looks tired, weak and thin.
2 She is saying that the cab is very heavy for the horse.
3 He is putting a lot of luggage on the cab.

Page 70 – exercise 3

1C 2A 3B 4B 5C

Chapter SEVEN

Page 78 – exercise 1

1A 2C 3B 4A 5B 6A

Page 79 – exercise 2

1 in 2 with 3 outside 4 about 5 for
6 under 7 on 8 at 9 up 10 in

Page 79 – exercise 3

1 His 2 with 3 him 4 is 5 to 6 and
7 with 8 you 9 your 10 at

Page 80 – exercise 4

1A 2C 3A 4C 5A

Recording script
Ellen and Mr Turner meet at the baker's. Ellen is buying biscuits and a chocolate cake.
Ellen: Hello, Mr Turner. It's good to see you.

Mr Turner: Hello Ellen, nice to see you too. Are you looking for a good horse?

Ellen: Yes, I'm looking for a gentle horse.

Mr Turner: I have a wonderful horse for you. His name is Black Beauty and he's five years old. He's very gentle and he's perfect for a lady.

Ellen: When can I see him?

Mr Turner: I can bring him to your house next week on Tuesday.

Ellen: That's good! Come in the morning before lunch.

Mr Turner: Where do you live?

Ellen: I live in the big white house near the river. How much does the horse cost?

Mr Turner: I can sell him to you for 18 pounds.

Page 81 – exercise 5

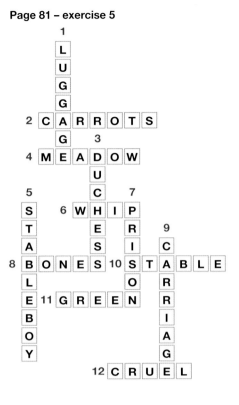

Page 82 – exercise 1

1A **2**A **3**B **4**B **5**C **6**A **7**B **8**A
9B **10**C **11**A **12**A **13**A

Page 83 – exercise 2

1H **2**F **3**K **4**A **5**I **6**B **7**C **8**G
9L **10**E **11**D **12**J

Page 84 – exercise 1

1 Anna Sewell
2 British
3 Royal Society for the Prevention of Cruelty to Animals. It helps and protects animals.
4 three types
5 Thoroughbred, American Saddle, Arabian Stallion, Quarter, Lipizzaner, Draft, Clydesdale, Shire, Percheron, Shetland, Welsh, Dartmoor.
6 oats, carrots, apples
7 It is a famous riding school in Vienna, Austria.

Page 84 – exercise 2

1 T
2 F – Black Beauty likes carrying his master.
3 T
4 F – Black Beauty is Lady Anne's favourite horse.
5 T
6 F – Mr Barry is a kind master but he knows nothing about horses.
7 T
8 T
9 T
10 F – Ellen Blomefield and her sisters keep Black Beauty forever.

Page 84 – exercise 3

1E **2**D **3**C **4**B **5**A **6**I **7**H **8**G **9**F

Page 85 – exercise 4

1 with **2** in **3** at **4** across **5** about
6 for **7** on **8** up **9** under

Page 85 – exercise 5

Open answer

NOTES

 NOTES

NOTES

Black Cat English Readers

BLACK CAT ENGLISH CLUB
Membership Application Form

BLACK CAT ENGLISH CLUB is for those who love English reading and seek for better English to share and learn with fun together.

Benefits offered: - *Membership Card*
   - *Member badge, poster, bookmark*
   - *Book discount coupon*
   - *Black Cat English Reward Scheme*
   - *English learning e-forum*
   - *Surprise gift and more...*

Simply fill out the application form below and fax it back to 2565 1113.

Join Now! It's FREE exclusively for readers who have purchased *Black Cat English Readers* !

The book(or book set) that you have purchased: _____

English Name:_____ (Surname) _____ (Given Name)

Chinese Name: _____

Address:_____

Tel: _____ Fax: _____

Email:_____
Sex: ❏ Male   ❏ Female   (Login password for e-forum will be sent to this email address.)

Education Background: ❏ Primary 1-3   ❏ Primary 4-6   ❏ Junior Secondary Education (F1-3)
   ❏ Senior Secondary Education (F4-5)   ❏ Matriculation
   ❏ College   ❏ University or above

Age: ❏ 6 - 9   ❏ 10 - 12   ❏ 13 - 15   ❏ 16 - 18   ❏ 19 - 24   ❏ 25 - 34
   ❏ 35 - 44   ❏ 45 - 54   ❏ 55 or above

Occupation: ❏ Student   ❏ Teacher   ❏ White Collar   ❏ Blue Collar
   ❏ Professional   ❏ Manager   ❏ Business Owner   ❏ Housewife
   ❏ Others (please specify: _____)

As a member, what would you like **BLACK CAT ENGLISH CLUB** to offer:

❏ Member gathering/ party   ❏ English class with native teacher   ❏ English competition
❏ Newsletter   ❏ Online sharing   ❏ Book fair
❏ Book discount   ❏ Others (please specify: _____)

Other suggestions to **BLACK CAT ENGLISH CLUB**:

_____

Please sign here: _____

(Date: _____)